Priceless Gifts
A Folktale from Italy

Martha Hamilton & Mitch Weiss

Illustrated by
John Kanzler

AUGUST HOUSE
Little folk

ATLANTA

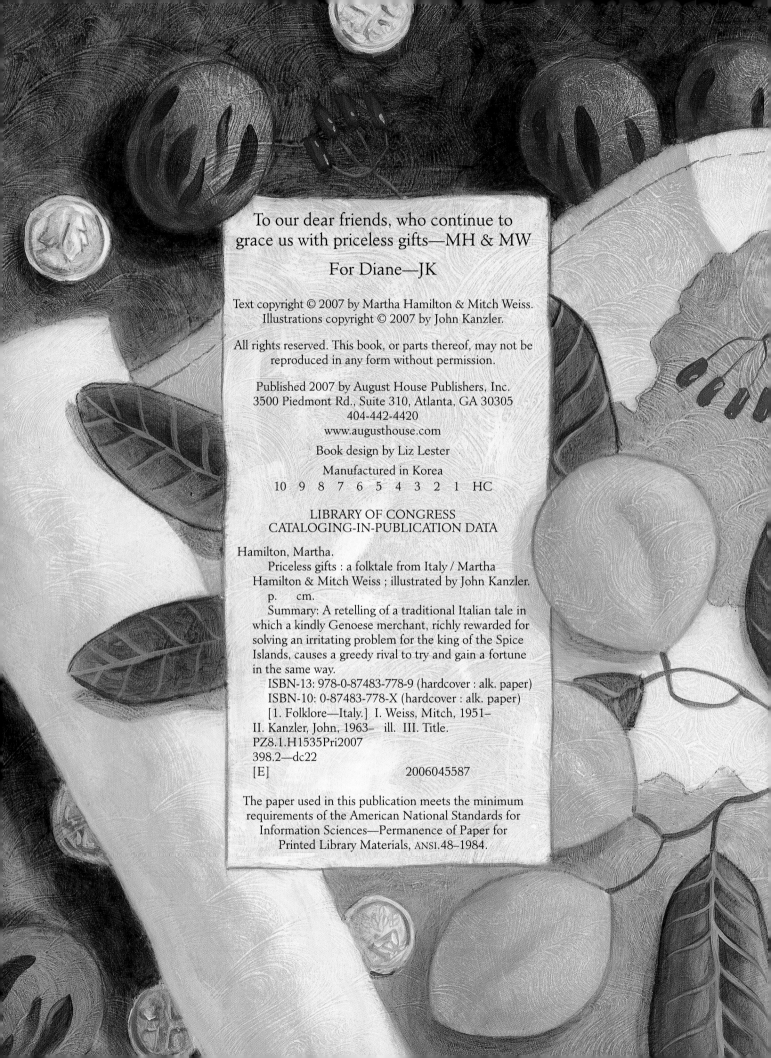

To our dear friends, who continue to
grace us with priceless gifts—MH & MW

For Diane—JK

Text copyright © 2007 by Martha Hamilton & Mitch Weiss.
Illustrations copyright © 2007 by John Kanzler.

Published 2007 by August House Publishers, Inc.
3500 Piedmont Rd., Suite 310, Atlanta, GA 30305
404-442-4420
www.augusthouse.com

Book design by Liz Lester

Manufactured in Korea
10 9 8 7 6 5 4 3 2 1 HC

LIBRARY OF CONGRESS
CATALOGING-IN-PUBLICATION DATA

Hamilton, Martha.
    Priceless gifts : a folktale from Italy / Martha
Hamilton & Mitch Weiss ; illustrated by John Kanzler.
    p.   cm.
    Summary: A retelling of a traditional Italian tale in
which a kindly Genoese merchant, richly rewarded for
solving an irritating problem for the king of the Spice
Islands, causes a greedy rival to try and gain a fortune
in the same way.
    ISBN-13: 978-0-87483-778-9 (hardcover : alk. paper)
    ISBN-10: 0-87483-778-X (hardcover : alk. paper)
    [1. Folklore—Italy.] I. Weiss, Mitch, 1951–
II. Kanzler, John, 1963– ill. III. Title.
PZ8.1.H1535Pri2007
398.2—dc22
[E]   2006045587

The paper used in this publication meets the minimum
requirements of the American National Standards for
Information Sciences—Permanence of Paper for
Printed Library Materials, ANSI.48–1984.

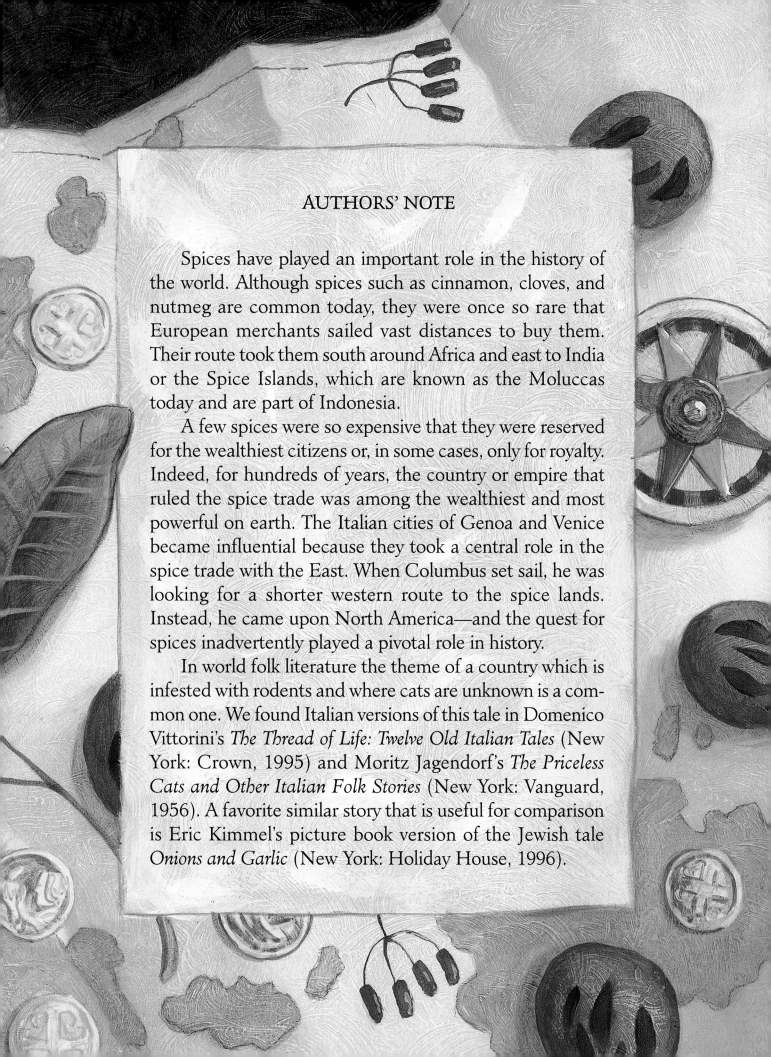

AUTHORS' NOTE

Spices have played an important role in the history of the world. Although spices such as cinnamon, cloves, and nutmeg are common today, they were once so rare that European merchants sailed vast distances to buy them. Their route took them south around Africa and east to India or the Spice Islands, which are known as the Moluccas today and are part of Indonesia.

A few spices were so expensive that they were reserved for the wealthiest citizens or, in some cases, only for royalty. Indeed, for hundreds of years, the country or empire that ruled the spice trade was among the wealthiest and most powerful on earth. The Italian cities of Genoa and Venice became influential because they took a central role in the spice trade with the East. When Columbus set sail, he was looking for a shorter western route to the spice lands. Instead, he came upon North America—and the quest for spices inadvertently played a pivotal role in history.

In world folk literature the theme of a country which is infested with rodents and where cats are unknown is a common one. We found Italian versions of this tale in Domenico Vittorini's *The Thread of Life: Twelve Old Italian Tales* (New York: Crown, 1995) and Moritz Jagendorf's *The Priceless Cats and Other Italian Folk Stories* (New York: Vanguard, 1956). A favorite similar story that is useful for comparison is Eric Kimmel's picture book version of the Jewish tale *Onions and Garlic* (New York: Holiday House, 1996).

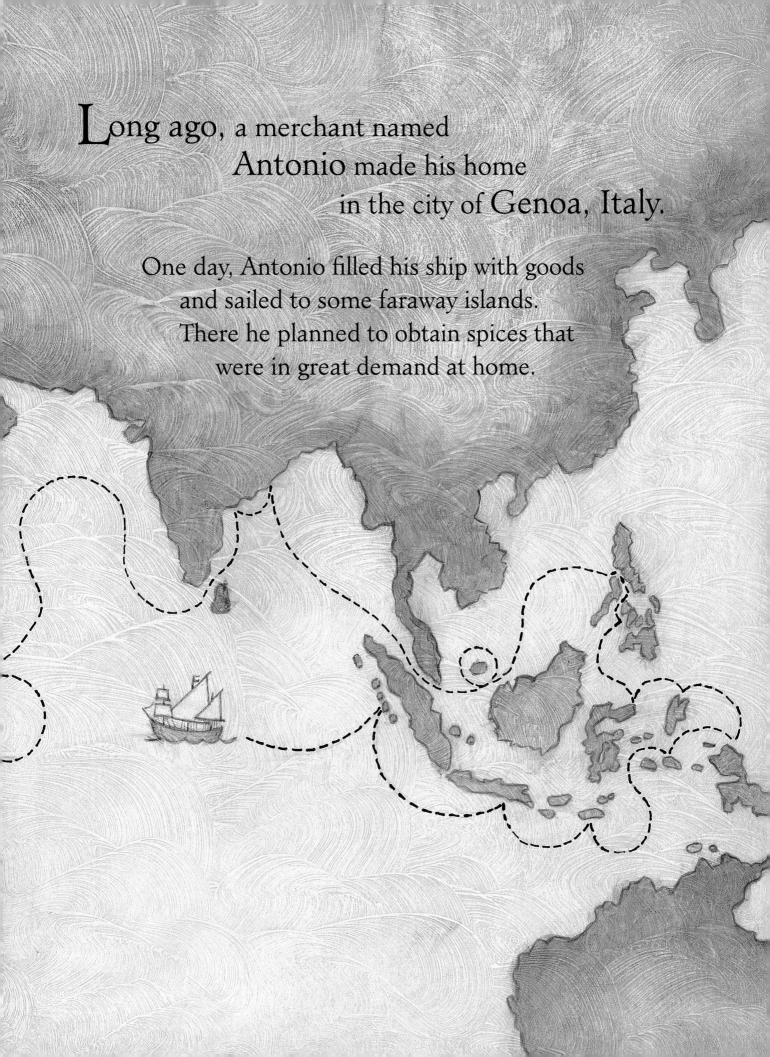

Long ago, a merchant named
Antonio made his home
in the city of Genoa, Italy.

One day, Antonio filled his ship with goods
and sailed to some faraway islands.
There he planned to obtain spices that
were in great demand at home.

When he arrived, Antonio
traveled from island to island.

He traded
velvet for cinnamon,
dolls for cloves,
and leather belts for nutmeg.

On one island, Antonio was invited to dine at the king's palace.

But when he sat down to eat, Antonio saw several men holding sticks as if they were ready to strike something.

"How strange!" he wondered.

"What are these guards doing?"

Antonio's question was answered when
dinner was served.

Attracted by the smell of food,
dozens of rats suddenly appeared.

The guards chased the rats
this way and that and
drove them away
with the sticks.

Antonio was horrified. "Your Majesty," he said, "don't you have cats on this island?"

The king looked baffled.

"Cats? Never heard of them. What are they?"

"Cats are small, furry animals that love to hunt," replied Antonio.

"More than anything else, they like to chase rats. They would rid this island of rodents in no time!"

"Really?" asked the king.
"Where might we find some cats?
If you bring us some, we will pay anything
for them! Just name your price."

"It is not necessary to pay me for cats," Antonio explained.
"We have many on our ship. I am happy to give
you some."

Antonio left and returned quickly with a female tabby
and a male tomcat. When he set them loose, the
rats scurried from the dining hall, with
the cats close at their heels.

"What amazing
animals!"
cried the king.

"Thank you, my friend. Now, I would like to give you something in return."

The king presented Antonio with a chest filled with precious stones and gleaming jewels.

"Your Majesty, there is no need for this," protested Antonio. But the king would not take no for an answer. "Antonio, you have given us a priceless gift. Besides, we have so many gems and jewels on our island that we don't know what to do with them.

Please accept this present in exchange for these truly fine animals."

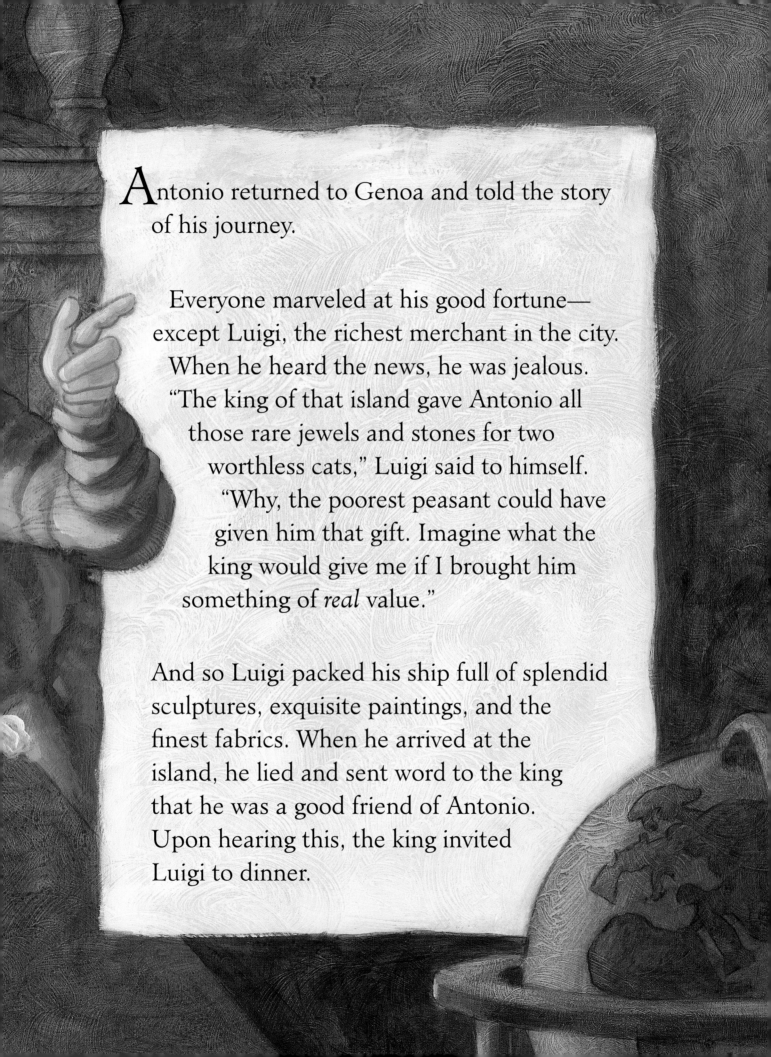

Antonio returned to Genoa and told the story of his journey.

Everyone marveled at his good fortune—except Luigi, the richest merchant in the city. When he heard the news, he was jealous. "The king of that island gave Antonio all those rare jewels and stones for two worthless cats," Luigi said to himself. "Why, the poorest peasant could have given him that gift. Imagine what the king would give me if I brought him something of *real* value."

And so Luigi packed his ship full of splendid sculptures, exquisite paintings, and the finest fabrics. When he arrived at the island, he lied and sent word to the king that he was a good friend of Antonio. Upon hearing this, the king invited Luigi to dinner.

When he saw the treasures,
the king was stunned.

"I am touched by your generosity,
Luigi," he declared. "I don't
know how I can repay you."

The king met with his counselors. After some time, Luigi was called to the royal chamber.

"We have debated at length about a present for you, Luigi. I am pleased to say that we have finally come up with the perfect one. It is truly priceless."

With that, the king ordered his servants to bring in the gift.

Luigi could barely contain his excitement.

He was certain he would receive at least twenty times as many jewels as Antonio.

The king presented Luigi with a silken cushion covered with a velvet cloth.

When Luigi lifted the cloth, he was speechless.

There sat a ball of fur.

When it moved, Luigi realized that it was . . .

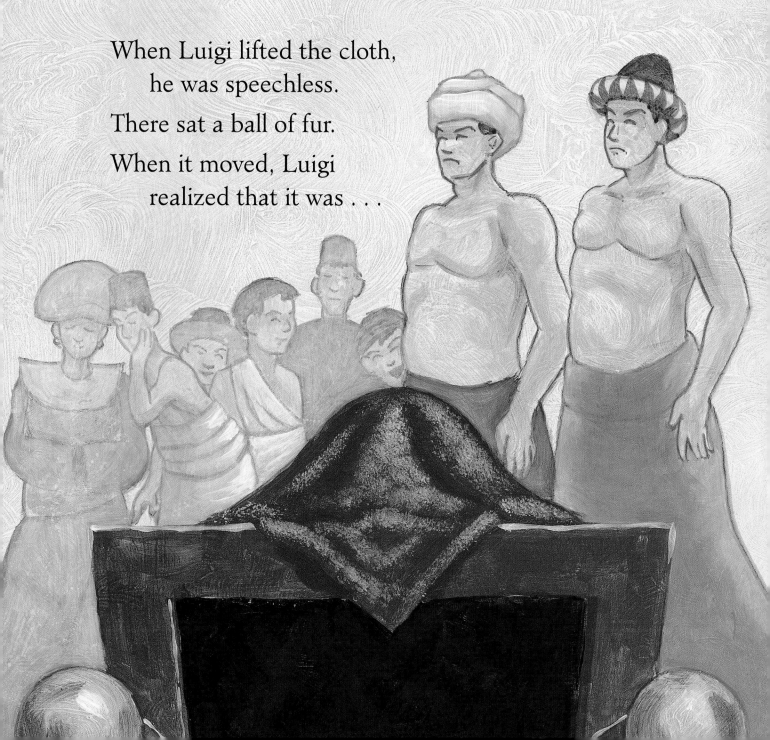

... a kitten.

"The priceless cats that
your friend Antonio gave
us just had a litter of
kittens. Because you
blessed us with such lavish
gifts, we wanted to pay
you with our most
precious possession."

As Luigi looked at the beaming face of the king, he realized that, in the king's mind, the little kitten was worth far more than all the treasures Luigi had given to him.

He knew the right thing to do was smile and pretend to be delighted with the gift, and that's what he did.

And although Luigi did not return home a richer man, he was certainly a wiser one.